Who's a Goblin?

written by Dandi
illustrated by Mark Clapsadle

I thought I saw a goblin,
But I guess it was the moon.
Anyway, my mama says
She'll get my costume soon.

It's time to put my costume on.

I think I'll be a ghost.

I'd never be a goblin!

It's the thing I fear the most.

I thought I heard a goblin,
But it might have been the wind.
'Cause when I told my mother,
She just looked at me and grinned.

My friend and I will trick or treat.

I'm glad I'm not alone.

For just beyond that big, black cat

I thought I heard a moan.

There's something in the bushes!

Yes, I think I saw it move.

I'd like to tell my buddy,

But it's pretty hard to prove.

I think I smell a goblin —
Something horrible and old.
I maybe should investigate,
But I'm really not that bold!

"Trick or Treat!" we shouted,
As we begged for all the sweets.
I spied a chocolate goblin
Underneath the other treats!

I fear a goblin's watching,
So I ask my friend to hurry.
I peek around the corner,
But my friend says not to worry.

I think I feel a goblin,
And I think I feel him near.
Just one more house to visit,
Then that's it until next year!

All the way home –
I think I sense a goblin chasing me.
I shed my sheet, and run for home
As fast as I can flee.

I'm done with trick or treating.
I dump out all my loot.
I stuff my face with candy,
A cookie, and some fruit.

My mom walks in and sees me eat.

She says, "All that from trick or treat?

My how you gobble!" Then I see –

The only GOBLIN here is ME!